Cricket Song

Cricket Song

Written and illustrated by
Anne Hunter

HOUGHTON MIFFLIN HARCOURT
Boston   New York

To my mother, for taking us into the wilds.

www.hmhco.com

The text of this book is set in McKenna Handletter and Adorn Pomander.
The illustrations are done in watercolor and ink.

Library of Congress Cataloging-in-Publication Data
Hunter, Anne, author, illustrator.
Cricket song / written and illustrated by Anne Hunter.
pages cm
Summary: As crickets sing in the breeze, hunting owls watch over the
bay, and sea otters doze on the tide, two children on different
continents go to bed.
ISBN 978-0-544-58259-0
[1. Bedtime—Fiction. 2. Animals—Fiction.] I. Title.
PZ7.H916555Cr 2016
2014048561

Manufactured in China
SCP 10 9 8 7 6 5 4 3 2 1
4500560897

As the sun sails west, bringing
the night, the evening breeze
rises to meet it.

The breeze carries the song
of crickets into your room.

Out in the yard, cricket-song mingles with the *kreck kreck kreck* of frogs in the stream.

The frogs puff their
throats full of cool air
from the woods,

where the poorwill
calls *poorwill! poorwill!* and
listens for the footfall of the fox.

The fox sniffs for the
scent of the rabbit,

who hides in her hole in the field,
listening to the *hoo, hoo, hoo* of a hunting owl
carried on the ocean air.

The owl watches over the bay,
where drifting sea otters doze

on the tide that carries a rumble from
the whales singing deep in the sea.

The whales rise up to breathe in
air warmed by another land

that smells of the suppers of fishermen
who beach their boats for the night

and hurry home to the *scrawk, scrawk* of parakeets who roost in the tree

that grows in the yard of a child

who dozes, like you,
to the song of crickets

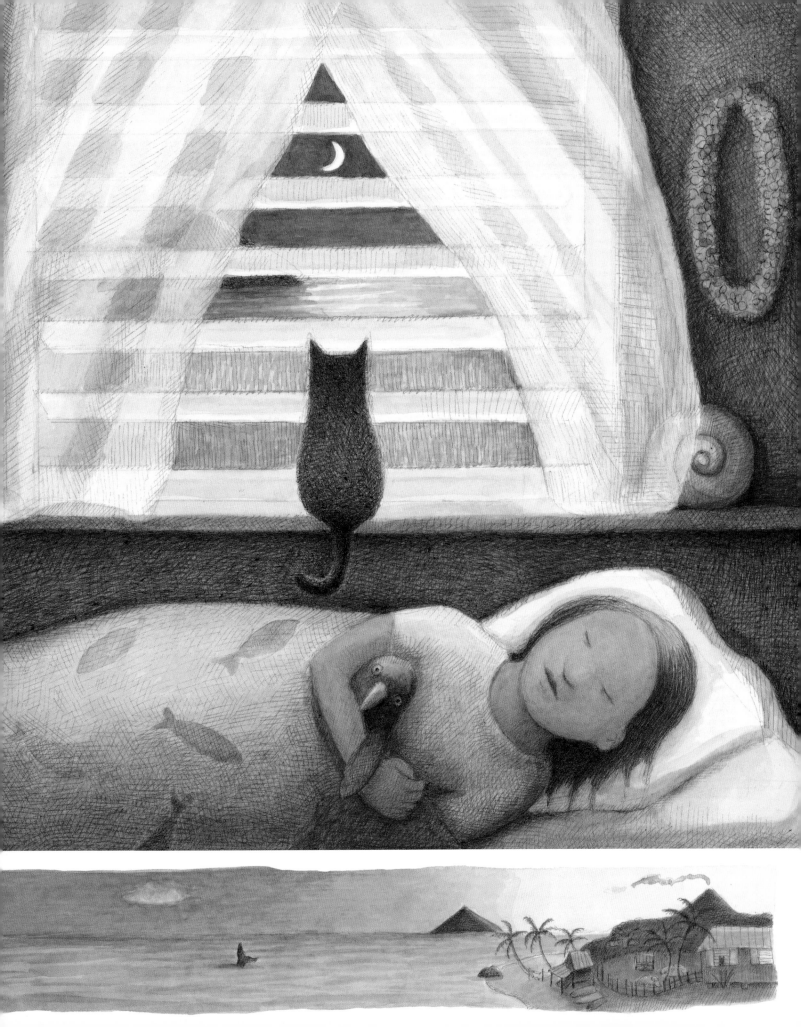

brought on the evening breeze.